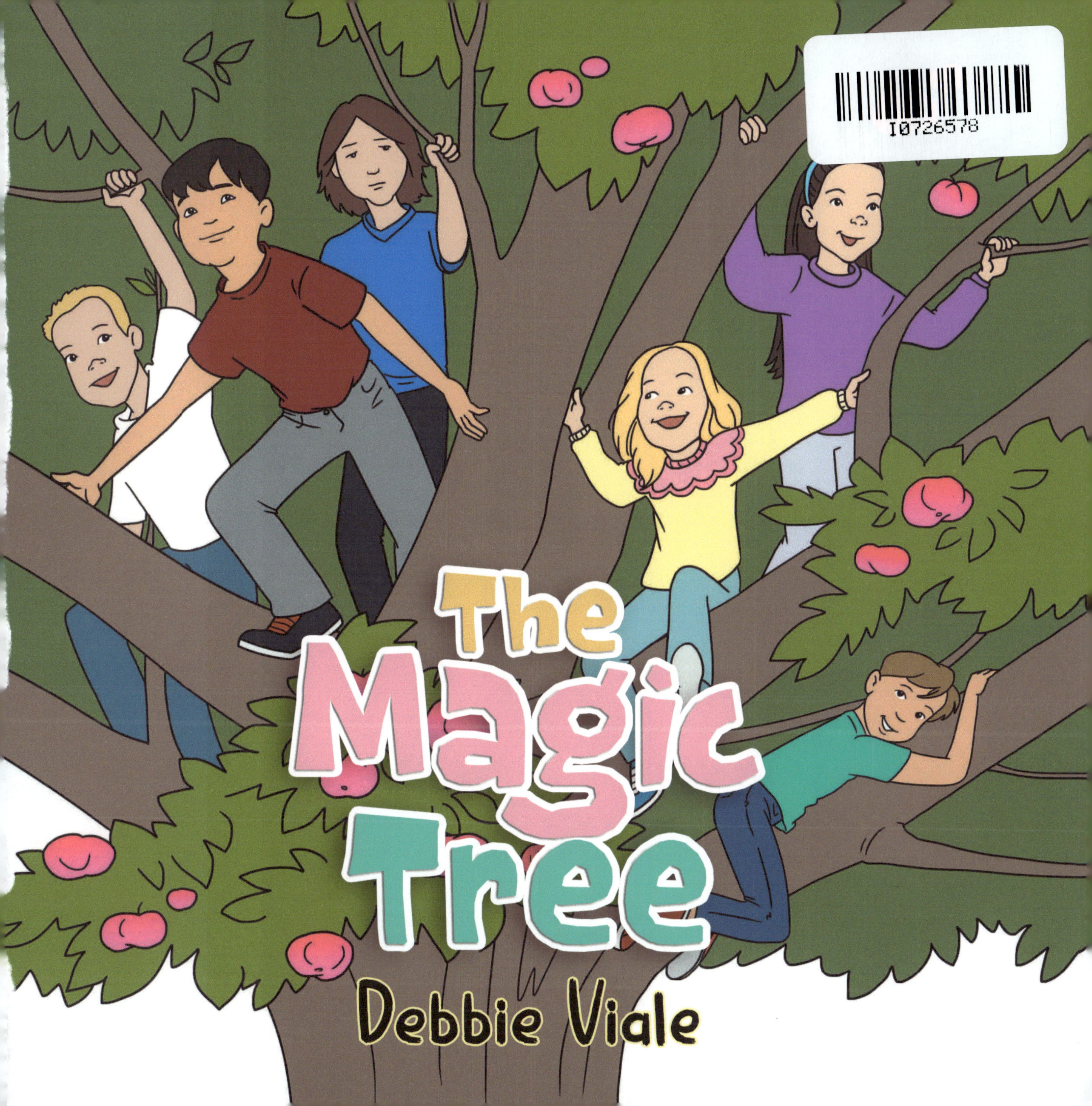

The Magic Tree
Debbie Viale

Copyright © 2022 by Debbie Viale

Hardcover: 978-1-958381-28-1
Paperback: 978-1-958381-07-6
eBook: 978-1-958381-06-9
Library of Congress Control Number: 2022910693

This is a work of fiction.

The
Magic
Tree

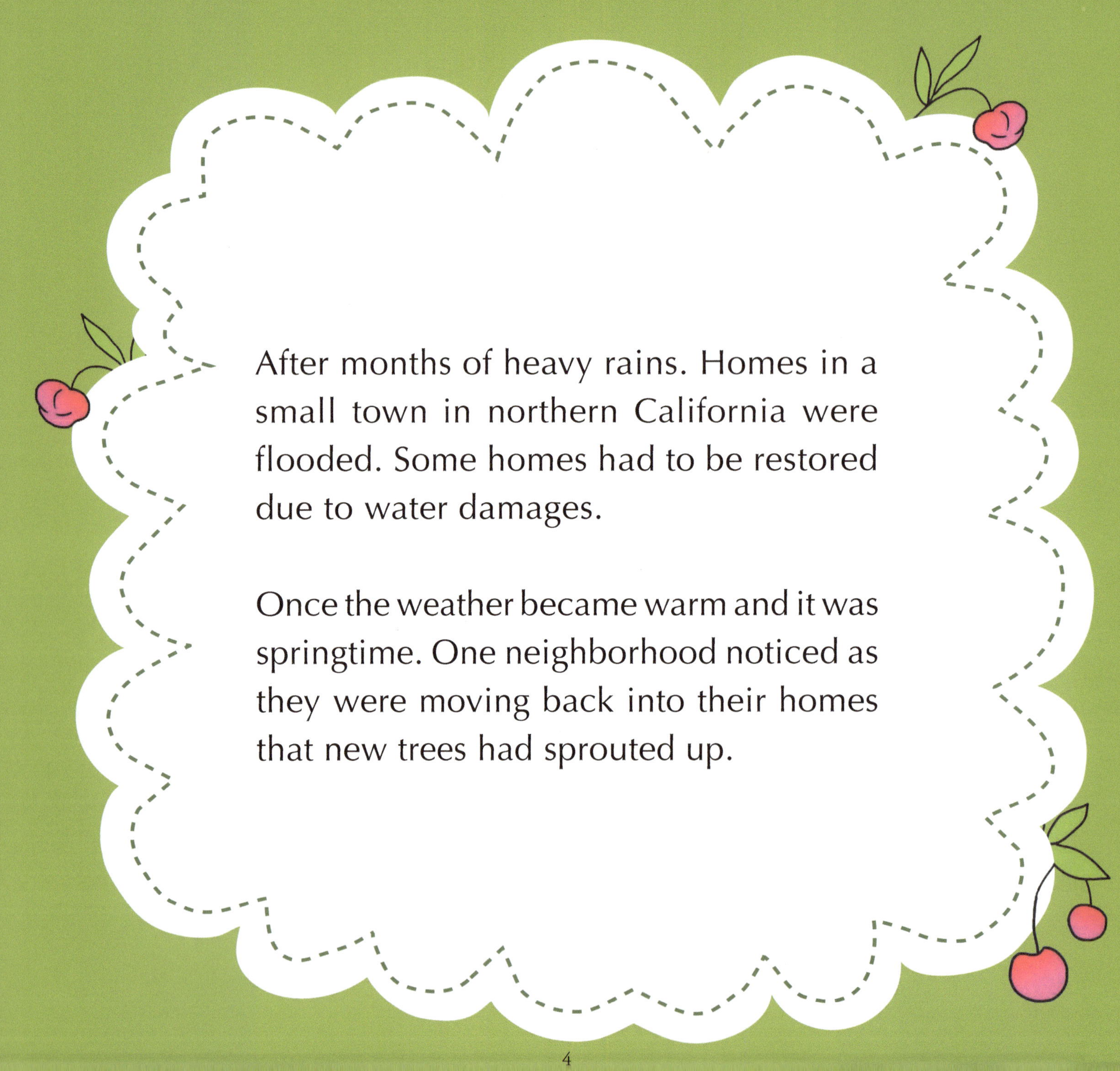

After months of heavy rains. Homes in a small town in northern California were flooded. Some homes had to be restored due to water damages.

Once the weather became warm and it was springtime. One neighborhood noticed as they were moving back into their homes that new trees had sprouted up.

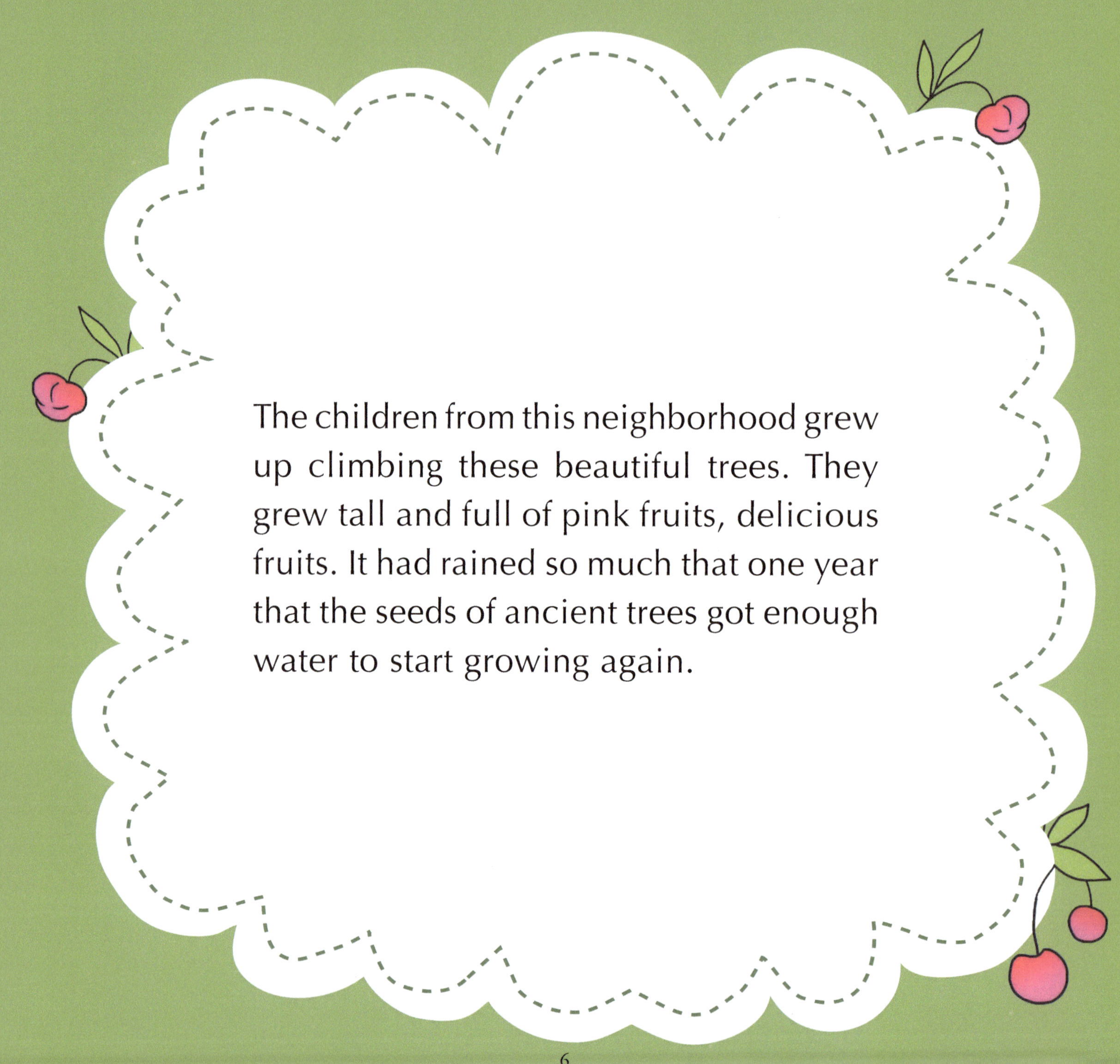

The children from this neighborhood grew up climbing these beautiful trees. They grew tall and full of pink fruits, delicious fruits. It had rained so much that one year that the seeds of ancient trees got enough water to start growing again.

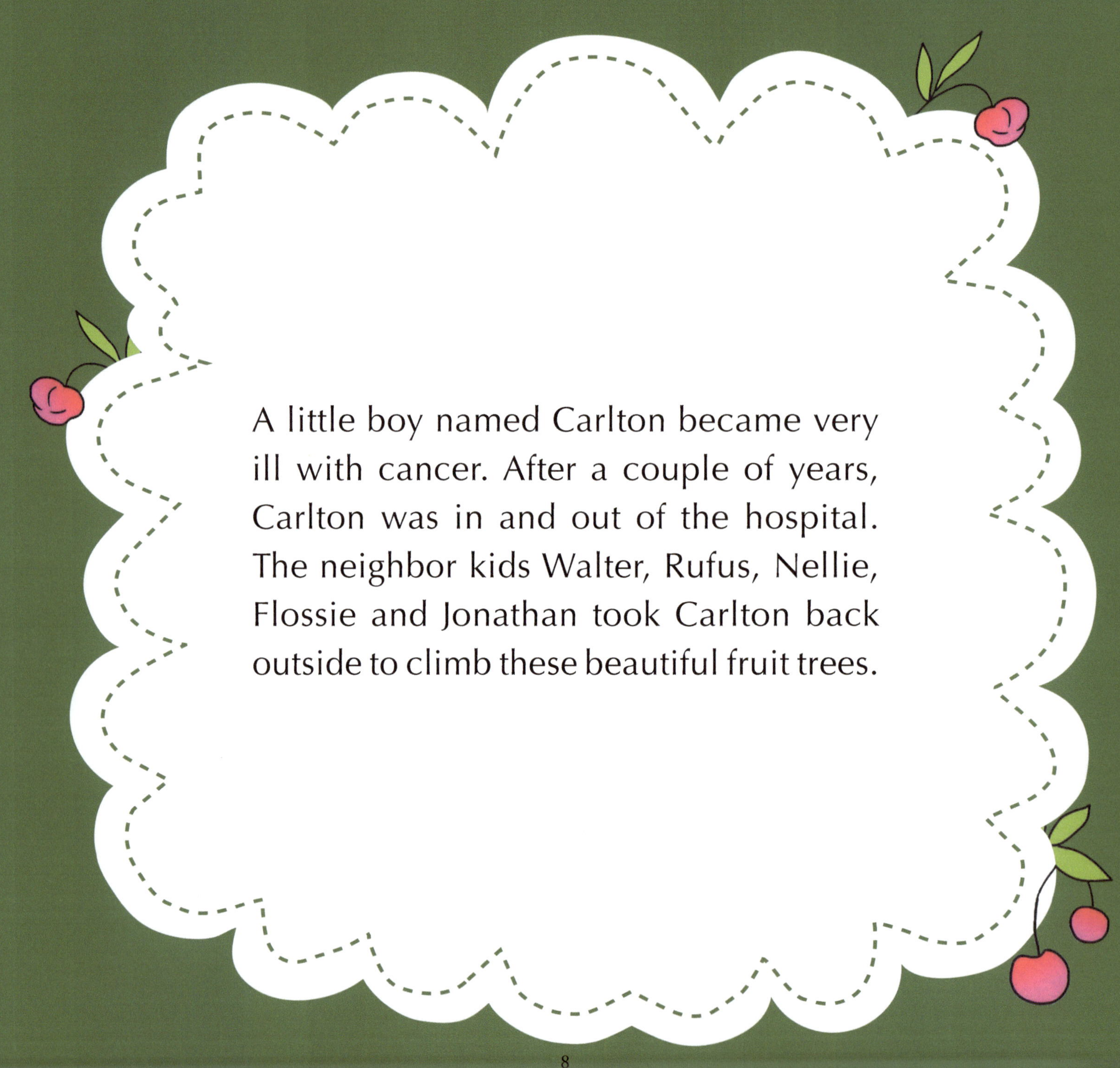

A little boy named Carlton became very ill with cancer. After a couple of years, Carlton was in and out of the hospital. The neighbor kids Walter, Rufus, Nellie, Flossie and Jonathan took Carlton back outside to climb these beautiful fruit trees.

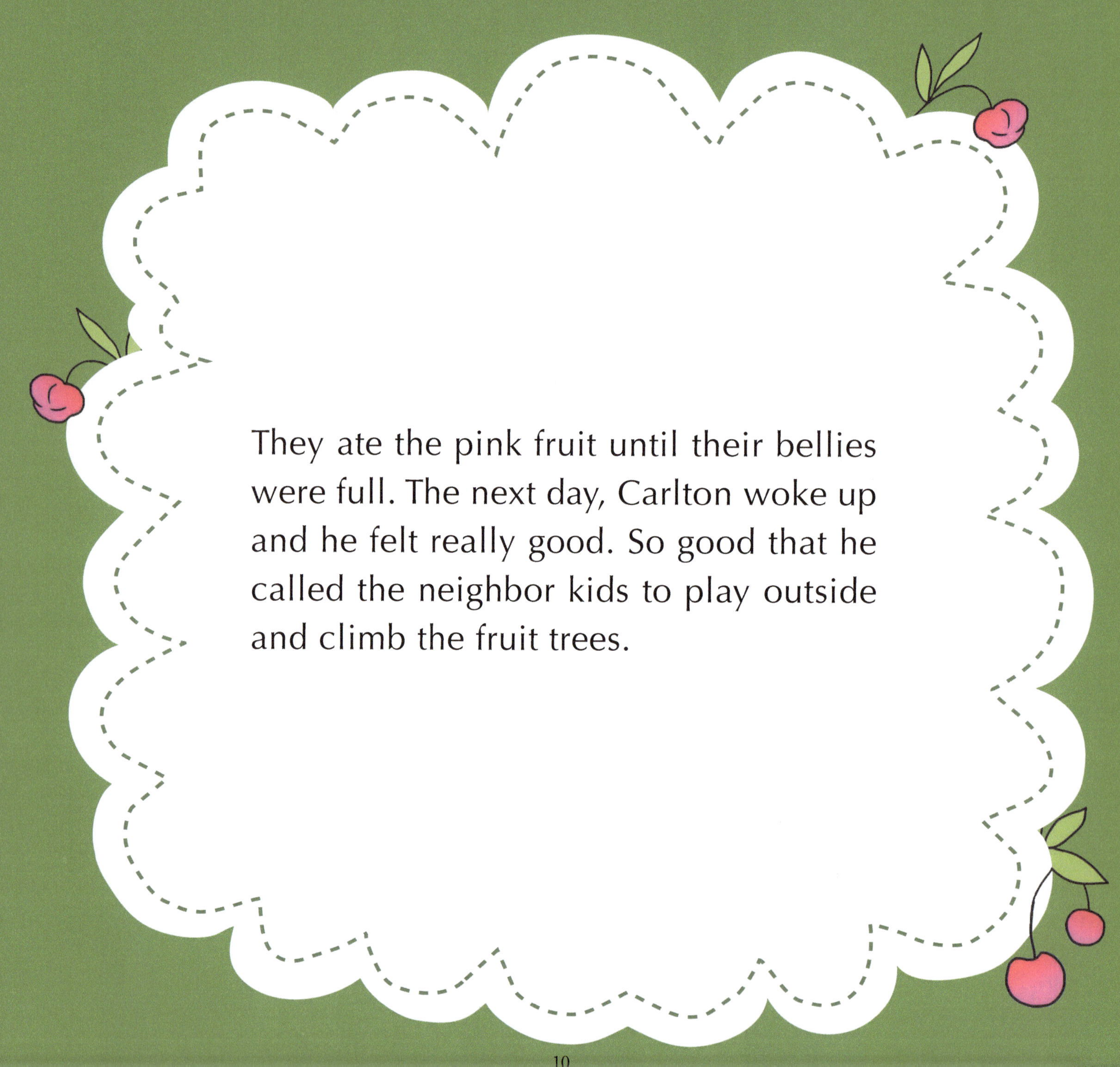

They ate the pink fruit until their bellies were full. The next day, Carlton woke up and he felt really good. So good that he called the neighbor kids to play outside and climb the fruit trees.

Flossie fell out of the tree and hit her head, which knocked her out cold.

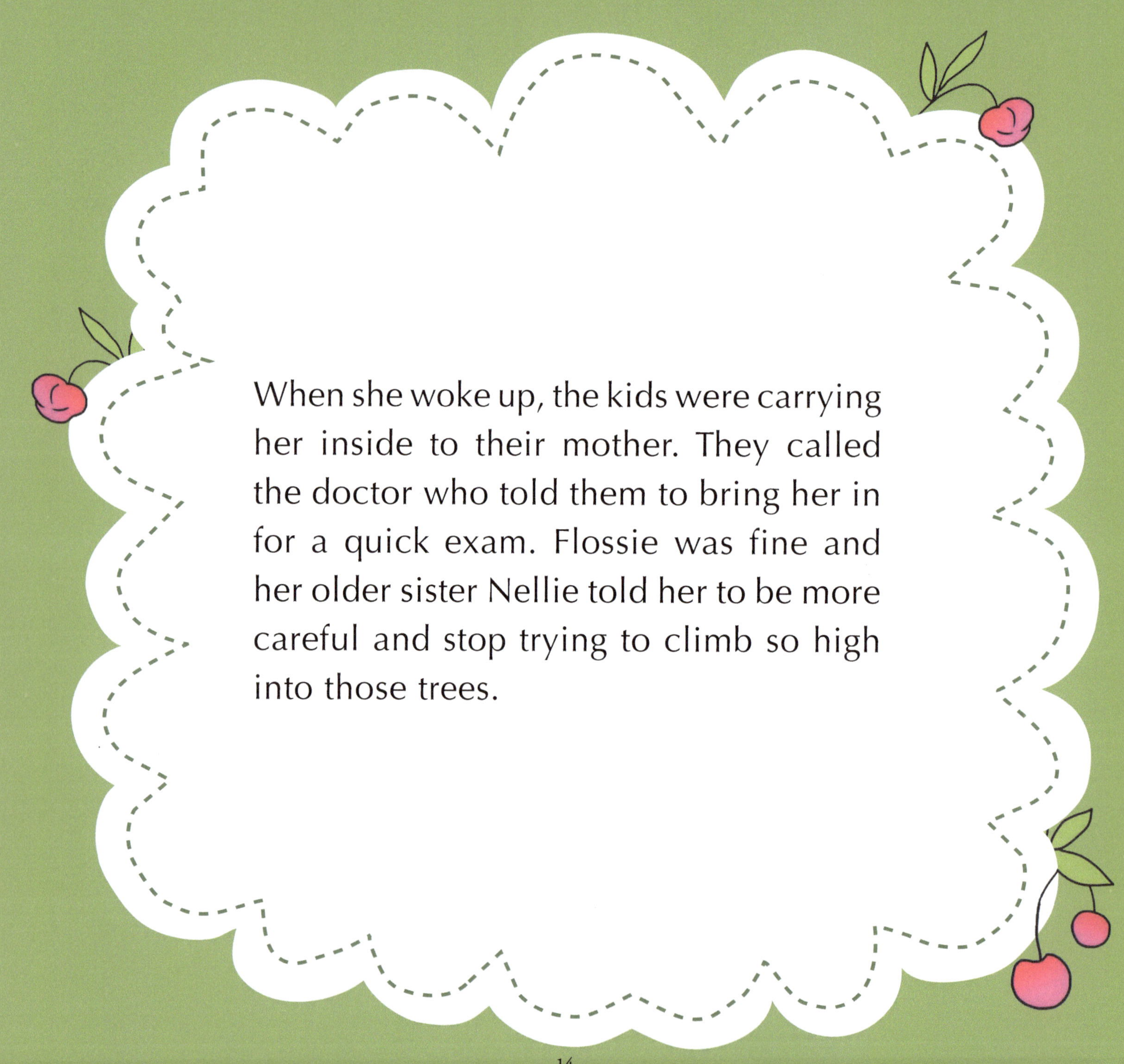

When she woke up, the kids were carrying her inside to their mother. They called the doctor who told them to bring her in for a quick exam. Flossie was fine and her older sister Nellie told her to be more careful and stop trying to climb so high into those trees.

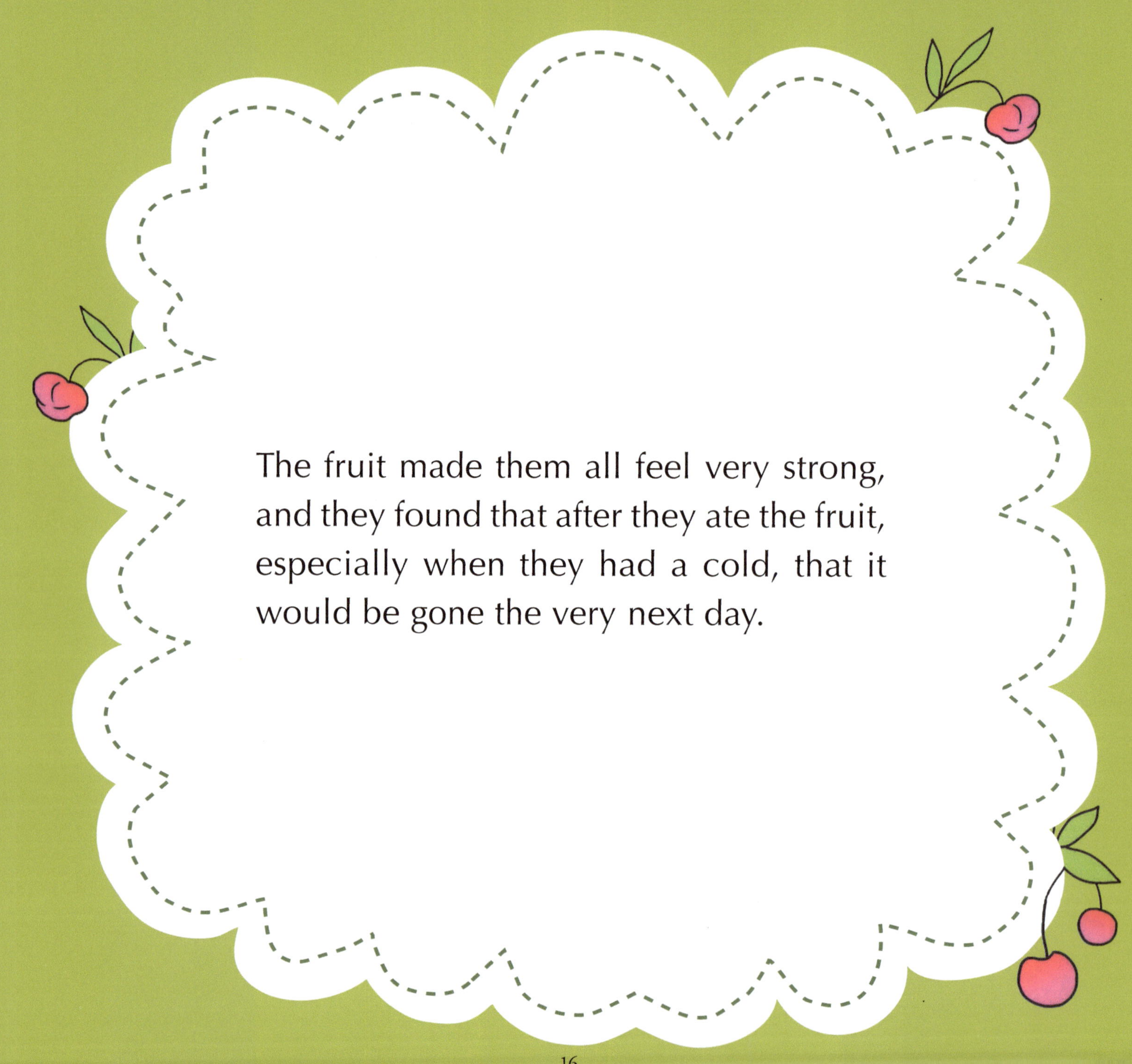

The fruit made them all feel very strong, and they found that after they ate the fruit, especially when they had a cold, that it would be gone the very next day.

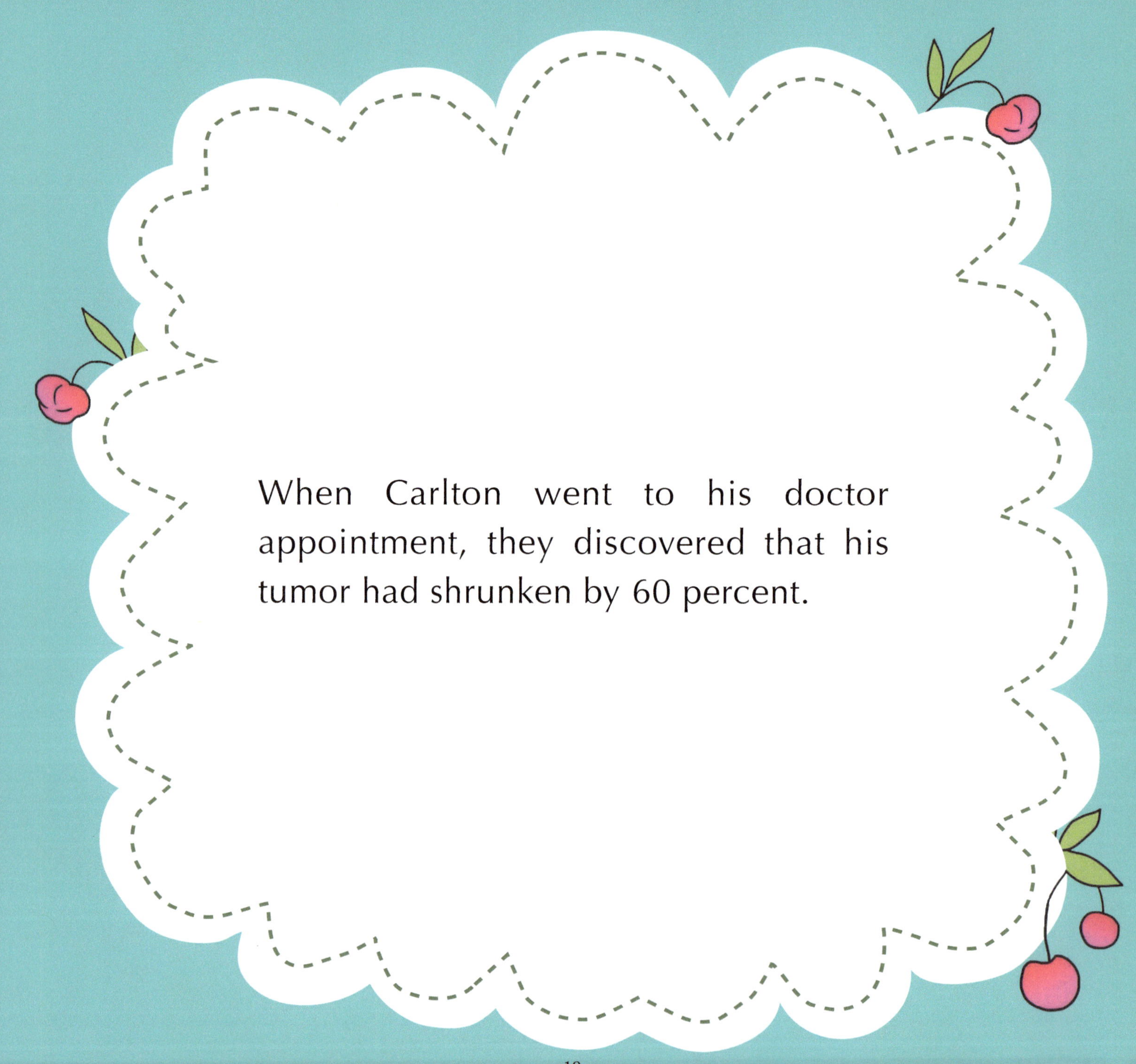

When Carlton went to his doctor appointment, they discovered that his tumor had shrunken by 60 percent.

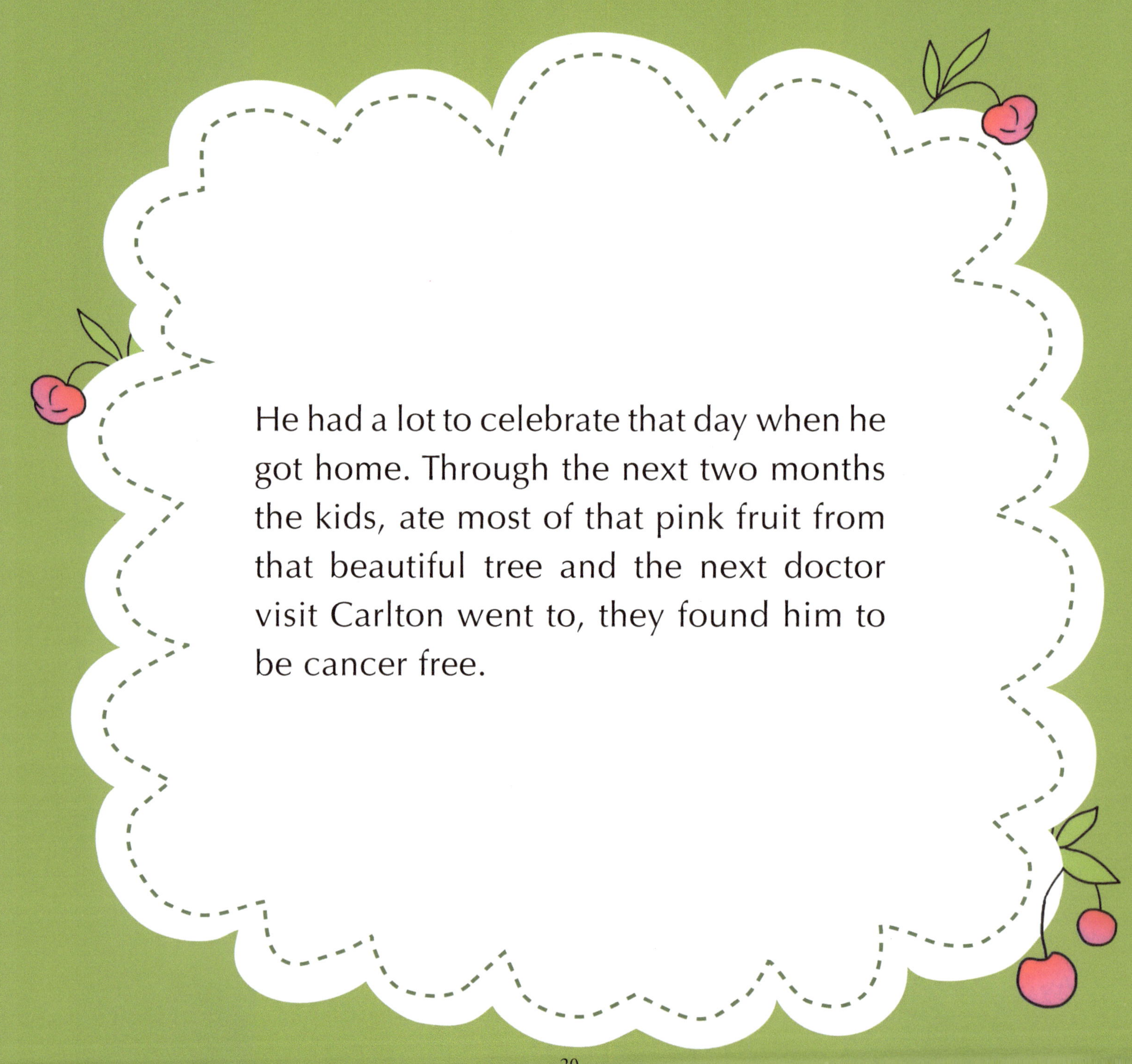

He had a lot to celebrate that day when he got home. Through the next two months the kids, ate most of that pink fruit from that beautiful tree and the next doctor visit Carlton went to, they found him to be cancer free.

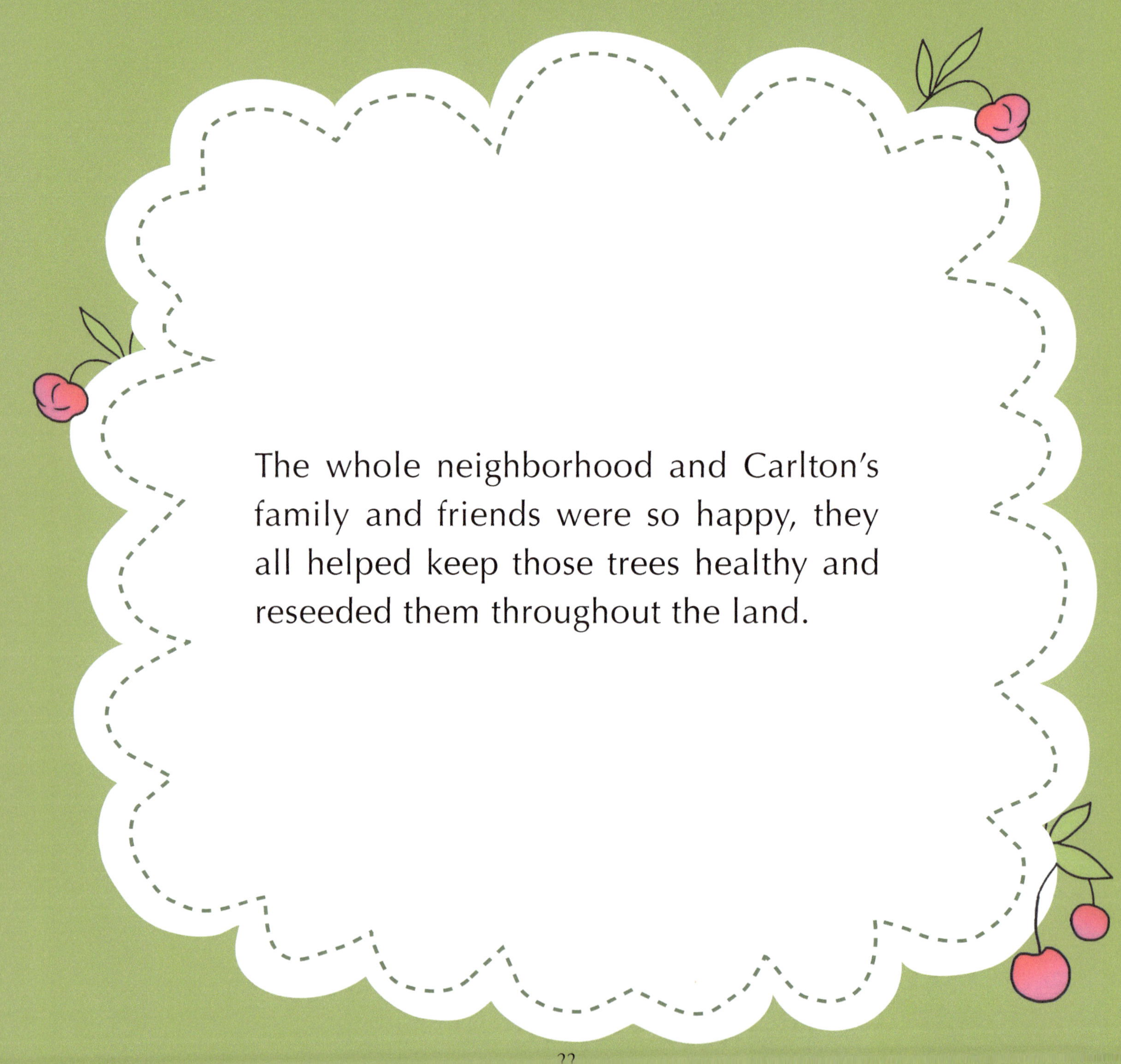

The whole neighborhood and Carlton's family and friends were so happy, they all helped keep those trees healthy and reseeded them throughout the land.